First published in Germany by Verlag Friedrich Oetinger, Hamburg © 1997

This edition first published in the United Kingdom in 2007 by
The Chicken House, 2 Palmer Street, Frome, Somerset, BA11 1DS
www.doublecluck.com

Text © 1997 Cornelia Funke
Illustrations © 1997 Kerstin Meyer
Translation © 2007 Chantal Wright

Designed by Ian Butterworth

Printed and bound in China by Imago

British Library Cataloguing in Publication Data available
Library of Congress Cataloguing in Publication data available

Hardback ISBN: 978-1-905294-04-6
Paperback ISBN: 978-1-905294-32-9

PRINCESS PIGSTY

By Cornelia Funke Illustrated by Kerstin Meyer

Translated by Chantal Wright

Chicken House

2 Palmer Street, Frome, Somerset BA11 1DS

Drusilla, Rosalinda and Isabella were real princesses. Their beautiful clothes filled thirty wardrobes. They had footmen to blow their noses for them and ladies-in-waiting to tidy up their rooms, hang up their clothes and polish their crowns until they shone.

Every morning, three teachers taught them royal behaviour – how to sit on a throne without fidgeting, how to curtsey without falling over, how to yawn with your mouth closed and how to smile for a whole hour without taking a break.

Six footmen swept up the crumbs that fell from their plates, and six ladies-in-waiting made sure they didn't get the tiniest scratch whilst playing.

The princesses didn't feed their ponies and pet monkeys - oh no. They had three stable-hands to do that.

They even had three servants whose job it was to carry three cushions around, so that the royal behinds always had something soft to sit on.

What more could one wish for?

'Our children must be the happiest children in the world!' said their mother, the queen, every day.

But Isabella, the youngest princess, wasn't happy. Not one bit. Every night she sat by the window, looked up at the moon and sighed.

One morning Isabella jumped out of bed and shouted out in such a loud voice that the whole castle woke up:

'I am tired of being a princess! It's boring, boring, boring!'

Her older sisters looked up from their feather pillows in surprise.

'I want to get dirty!' cried Isabella, bouncing around on the bed. 'I want to blow my own nose. I don't want to smile all the time. I want to make my own sandwiches. I don't want to have my hair curled ever again. I do not want to be a princess any more!'

And with that, she took her crown and threw it out of the window. Splash! It landed in the goldfish pond.

'There'll be trouble now!' said Drusilla, and rang her bell.

The door flew open and in marched six servants.

'May we dress Your Highnesses for breakfast?' purred the head footman.

Rosalinda and Drusilla sat down in front of their mirrors straight away. But Isabella scrambled, quick as a flash, under her bed.

'Your Highness!' cried the head footman. 'I beg you come out from under there!'

'No, I don't want to be dressed!' Isabella called out. 'I don't want to have my hair curled. Yuckety yuk, I can't stand it. I'll wash myself. In the fish pond!'

'Yourself?' cried the footmen in horror. 'In the fish pond? Goodness gracious.'

And the head footman sent for the king right away.

ISABELLA!' thundered the king, in such a loud voice that his wig slipped out of place.

'Come out from under that bed immediately!'

'No!' replied Isabella. 'I don't want to be a princess any more. I'd rather starve down here.'

'Pull her out!' ordered the king. Isabella pinched and scratched and kicked, but it was no good. The footmen pulled her out by her feet and dressed her in her princess's dress.

'**W**here is your crown?' asked the king sternly.

'She threw it into the fish pond,' said Rosalinda.

'I most certainly did,' said Isabella. 'That thing gives me headaches. And you can't climb trees in this stupid dress. I want to wear trousers.'

'Princesses don't climb trees!' thundered the king.

'That's just it!' cried Isabella. 'Princesses don't do anything fun. Princesses don't even pick their noses. Princesses just stand around looking pretty. Yuck. I don't want to be a princess any more!'

'Fish your crown out of the pond this very minute!' cried the king.

'I will not!' Isabella shouted back. 'I'm never going to put that crown on ever again!'

The king stamped his foot. 'Take her to the kitchens! She shall wash dishes, clean pans, peel onions and scrub the oven until she fetches her crown from the fish pond!'

So the footmen took Isabella to the kitchens . . .

. . . and Isabella peeled potatoes, polished pans, plucked pheasants and whipped the cream that her sisters liked to eat for breakfast.

After three days her father sent for her.

'Isabella!' he sighed. 'You stink of onions.'

'So what?' said Isabella. 'Did you know that cream is made from milk?'

'No, I didn't know that,' groaned the king. 'Now, will you fetch your crown from the fish pond?'

'No,' said Isabella. 'What for?'

'Isabella!' cried the king, tearing both his wig and his crown from his head in rage. 'Off to the pigsty with you!'

So the footmen took Isabella to the pigsty . . .

. . . and Isabella helped feed the pigs and clean out the sty. The pigs nuzzled against her with their pink snouts, and Isabella scratched their bristly hides.

After three days her father sent for her again.

'Isabella!' he groaned. 'What do you look like?!'

'She stinks too!' cried her sisters.

'Did you know that pigs eat potatoes?' asked Isabella, pulling a piece of straw out of her hair. 'And that they're frightfully clever animals? It's a shame to eat them.'

'Isabella!' cried the king. 'For the last time will you now fetch your crown from the fish pond, put on a pretty dress and comb your hair?'

'No, I will not!' said Isabella. 'But I would like to help out some more in the pigsty.'

'Ugh!' cried her sisters, holding their noses. 'Then we don't want to share a room with her any longer!'

'I'd rather sleep in the straw anyway,' said Isabella. She fetched her favourite doll and her blanket and settled down in the pigsty.

When night came and the moon shone over the castle, the king crept out of his palace. He went to the fish pond and fished out his youngest daughter's crown. Then he went to find her in the pigsty.

'Oh my little daughter,' he said and sat down next to her on the straw.

'You are dirty and your hair feels like straw, but you look happy!'

'Yes, daddy!' said Isabella. 'I'm happier than I've ever been before in my entire life.'

'Good!' sighed the king. 'Here is your crown. You may do as you wish with it as long as you come back to the castle. I miss you.'

'I suppose I can wear it now and again,' said Isabella. 'Perhaps when I'm feeding the chickens or picking blackberries. Did you know that you can make jam out of blackberries?'

'No, I didn't know that,' said the king. 'But one of these days you can show me how it's done.'

He gave his daughter a big fat kiss on her dirty cheek, and she kissed him on his big fat nose. Then they walked back to the castle, hand in hand.

Isabella still sleeps in the pigsty rather a lot. She gave her fancy gowns to the cook's daughter, and as for curly hair . . .
Isabella never let anybody curl her hair EVER again!